The BONE TALKER

For Logan, Taylor, Landis, Tanner, Jacquelyn, Brandon, Jenna and for Kyara, who lives among the mountains in Switzerland. —SL

For all my prairie family, past and present, and especially for my sister Kathy, who was my western eyes. —BS

The BONE TALKER

by Shelley A. Leedahl   Illustrated by Bill Slavin

NORTHERN LIGHTS BOOKS FOR CHILDREN

Red Deer Press

Not so very long ago or far away lived an old woman whose life had wound down like a clock. Gone were the tick and tock of her youth, when she'd steered a raft down a roaring river and climbed the long arms of the trees. Now she creaked when she hobbled across the room.

She'd felt the passing of many seasons in her knees and had stopped marking the moons since her hair had spun into a white mist. Now the old woman talked to her bones as if they were her children, who also were old and scattered like dandelion seeds across the land.

"Shhh, shhh," she whispered when her bones began telling stories. "Give an old woman some peace."

The seasons turned, and turned again. The cold white dog of winter howled home, and spring flapped in beneath a robin's wing. The old woman's husband followed his feet outside to plant tomatoes and chat with neighbors over the garden's falling fence.

"How have you been?" they asked, for the winters were long and the wind had sharp teeth. The villagers burrowed inside their homes until the first blue crocuses blinked open.

"Not so good, not so bad," the old man answered. "I'm old."

"And how about Grandmother Bones?" they asked, for that is what the
village people had come to call the old woman, who no longer ventured outside.

"Not so good," the old man muttered. "Not so good."

One morning the neighbor on the east and the neighbor on the west met
in the middle. Together they stood at the gate of the old man and woman.

"The old woman is disappearing. Like words in the wind."

"Once they say she was quick as a hawk—"

"Keen as a fox—"

"Bright as a daisy."

"Now she's become like the water at the bottom of the well."

"We need to pull her up," they agreed. "The old man is not strong enough—"

"To do it alone."

So the neighbors and their families set out to make the old woman happy again. They brought her rich berry pies to tickle her tongue. The children made merry music to wake her sleeping feet. They carried stones like jewels to set in her windows and catch the afternoon sun, but the old woman did not tick or tock. Her tongue did not cluck with laughter and her feet did not dance in the dust. The shades of her eyes were often pulled.

"I thank you for your gifts," the old man assured his neighbors, "but my wife is tired and her thoughts are tangled. See how she sits there, talking to her bones?"

One by one all manner of men, women and children peeked around the door and glimpsed the old woman scolding an elbow. One by one they tiptoed away, unable to shape sense from her words.

The old man nodded and closed his door to the world outside.
He turned his beard toward the old woman, and his voice rose like a gust. "You do not speak except to your bones. My words roll over you like tumbleweeds. What is it you want? *Please* tell me. . . . What can I do?"

But the old woman said nothing—not a squawk or a babble or a squeak—and for that moment, even her bones stopped talking.

The old man patted her white mist of hair. "I wish," he crooned, "that you would climb down from the clouds."

The yellow drop of moon came out. The night sky filled with owls and echoes. Coyotes sang.

Inside their rooms and before their fires, the neighbors shuffled ideas about the old woman.

"We have our work and our families to fill the days," they contended. "The old man has his garden. But what does the old woman have?"

"She must have something, too."

"Not berry pies."

"Not merry music."

"Not stones that flash like diamonds."

They pooled their opinions like so many drops of rain, but none remained by morning light.

Time pushed on. The old man's tomatoes grew red and ripe, and the trees filled with green hearts. The children rolled into summer, and the colors of the land burst to life. Each day, the old man stirred the dirt around his tomatoes and the neighbors leaned across the garden fence.

"And how is Grandmother Bones today?" they inquired.

"Not so good," he confessed. "Not so good."

The neighbor on the west thought hard. The neighbor on the east thought harder. The old man thought hardest of all. Their thoughts met in the middle, and an idea bloomed like a wild pink rose.

"I am thinking—" said the neighbor on the east.

"That the old woman needs a pastime—" added the neighbor on the west.

"To keep her hands busy and fill the long brown hours of her days," finished the old man.

Once again the neighbors arrived at the old woman's door and the old man led them inside.

"I have beads and a string," one neighbor offered.

"Flowers from the valley to press beneath a stone," said another.

"Wheat to weave into women with golden dresses," tried a third.

The old woman swatted her knees for talking out of turn, and the neighbors raised their palms to the silent sky.

"She has closed her ears," they told the old man, "and our minds are dried up with thinking."

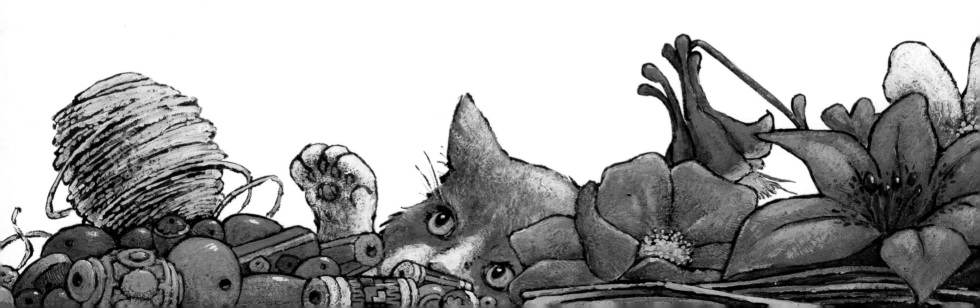

Just then a child crawled through the forest of legs to get close to the old woman. "Here," she offered. Her tiny hands held two bright pieces of cloth. "In your basket you have a needle and thread."

The old woman blinked and the neighbors gasped. She reached for the colored cloth and closed her crooked fingers around it.

"Bring me my basket," she drawled, as if tasting the flavor of each word for the first time or the last. The old man fetched the basket and set it on her lap. Everyone watched as she slowly and carefully slipped thread through the needle. She tied a knot in one end and stitched the two pieces of cloth together.

That was all. Then . . . "More."

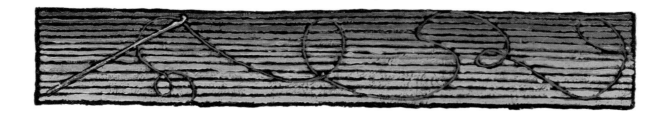

The villagers raced to their homes. The neighbor on the east plucked a
piece off her curtain. The neighbor on the west snatched a white patch of pocket. From every
direction, people returned waving small flags of color and hope. Grandmother Bones stitched and
stitched, and the old man's mouth curved toward a smile.

News of the old woman's revival reached each corner of the village. Soon other folks appeared at the old woman's doorstep with pieces of cloth and patches of memory in their hands.

"This was my daughter's first dress," explained one woman, offering a swatch of blue like a summer lake. The old woman thanked her and stitched it to the others. The light returned to her eyes.

A young boy brought the scrap of canvas he'd found in the crook of a tree. One family brought green ribbons that grew together like garden rows. Bits of apron and bites of leather were added here and there.

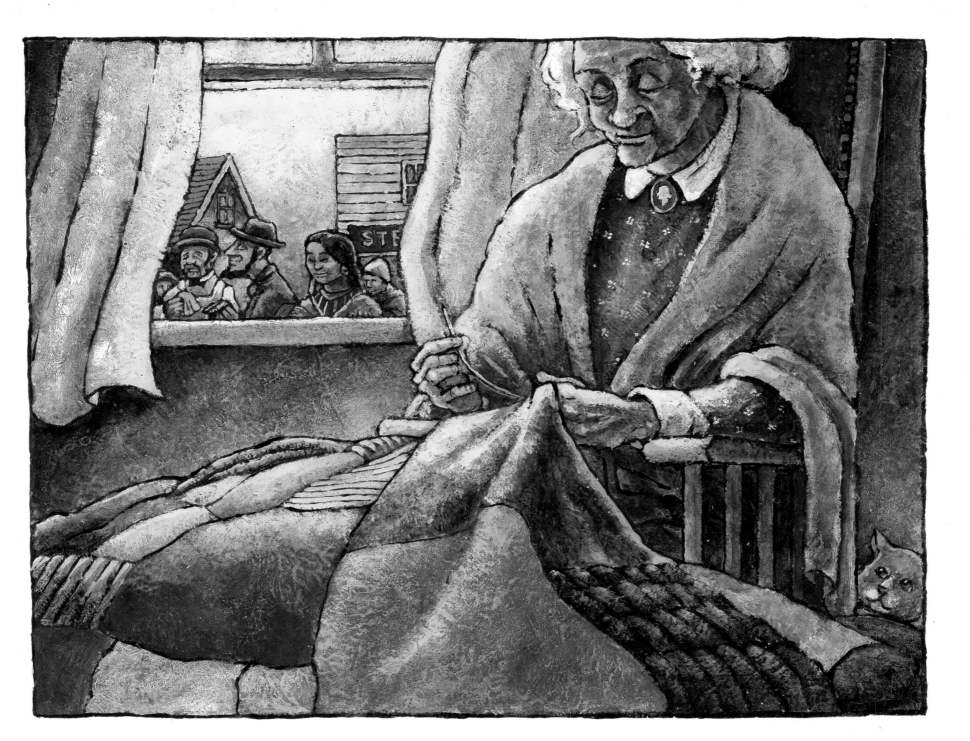

The tale caught onto the wind, and soon people from all across the land arrived with woolen rectangles and cotton rainbows. The old woman's hands flew like sparrows, and her laughter was heard well beyond her windows. Every night, the neighbors on the east and on the west fell asleep dreaming of her tick and tock.

One, three, nine, sixteen . . . Her children returned with their children and their children's children. They brought with them the fabric of their days, and from this the old woman learned the patterns of their lives.

The cloth filled the old couple's house, and Grandmother Bones waltzed it, yes, *waltzed* it—even with her old bones—right out the open front door. It flowed like a stream into the village, across the bridge and through the woods. It spread like a great cloak to the next village and the next and the next.

The old woman ticked and tocked long after her husband and neighbors had grown still themselves. No one knows when she stopped or when the giant cloth stopped growing. But if you fly through the prairie sky on a clear blue day and look way, way down, you'll see the old woman's work stretched right across the land.

Northern Lights Books for Children are published by
Red Deer Press
56 Avenue & 32 Street Box 5005
Red Deer Alberta Canada T4N 5H5

Acknowledgments
Edited for the Press by Peter Carver
Text design by Kunz+Associates Ltd.
Printed in Hong Kong for Red Deer Press

Financial support provided by the Alberta Foundation for the Arts, a beneficiary of the Lottery Fund of the Government of Alberta, and by the Canada Council, the Department of Canadian Heritage.

COMMITTED TO THE DEVELOPMENT OF CULTURE AND THE ARTS

Author's Acknowledgments
The first line of this book was given to me in a dream and discovering where it would lead was nothing but fun. I would like to extend special thanks to my mother, Helen Herr, who read the manuscript and responded with even more than her usual amount of enthusiasm; to Troy, chief meal-maker and husband extraordinaire; to Tim Wynne-Jones, who phoned one December afternoon to say he was rooting for the book; to Bill Slavin, who has the rare ability to enchant young and old alike with his superb illustrations; and to Peter Carver, for a painless, even enjoyable editing process.

Canadian Cataloguing in Publication Data
Leedahl, Shelley A. (Shelley Ann), 1963–
The bone talker
(Northern lights books for children)
ISBN 0-88995-214-0
I. Slavin, Bill. II. Title. III. Series.
PS8573.E3536B66 1999   jC813'.54   C99-910337-7
PZ7.L51522Bo 1999

5 4 3 2 I